Grandma's Silent Auction
April
BY: Michael James

Copyright © 2020 by Michael James

All rights reserved.

No part of this book may be reproduced in any form or by any electronic or mechanical means, including information storage and retrieval systems, without written permission from the author, except for the use of brief quotations in a book review.

CHAPTER ONE
CIARA

I step off the plane in Nevada and now that I've had time to think about what I am doing, I think I have lost my damn mind. I am not a bold in your face kind of girl. What I do need to do is unwind. I need to clear my head and let all these mixed up emotions in me settle down. I swear I am on the verge of losing my sanity. I should take these next couple of days and pull myself together. Before I can do that, I need to figure out where the hell I am staying. Leaving home was such a knee-jerk-reaction that I didn't plan anything out. I think in my head I was just going to show up at Kaiden's place and go from there. I see now that wasn't such a good idea. I need to find a hotel and lie low, then go from there. One thing that hasn't changed is the fact that I am not going to let him fall for me. By the end of this month, I hope he wishes he didn't waste his money on me. He'll wish he didn't outbid the guy below him.

I find my way out of the airport and wave down a taxi. I ask the guy if he can take me to the strip. I am pretty damn sure I will be able to find a place to stay there. Maybe I'll stay at a casino and do some gambling. Grams wants me to have an adventure, I might as well get started on my own, right?

As the driver drives us, I watch out the window. I've never been to Las Vegas before. It's interesting to see how much different it is here than at home. The neon lights are all you see. It is kind of fascinating to see firsthand.

"When would you like to get out?"

"Here is fine, I guess."

"Another block there are fine hotels."

"Okay, take me there."

We go the extra block and I get out. I scan the area. Which hotel should I pick? I see a doorman come outside, holding the door open for guests. I think to myself; that is inviting. I wait for the traffic light to change before I cross the street.

I wheel my luggage across the street to the hotel. When I reach the entrance, the doorman opens the door. I thank him as I enter. I get inside and it is really a beautiful hotel. There's a lounge to my right, then a hallway marked with a neon light that reads *Seven Jewels Casino*. To my left, there are elevators and a service desk. Seven Jewels Hotel it says. I wheel my suitcase behind me as I walk toward the front desk. I have a good feeling about this place.

"Welcome to Seven Jewels Hotel. How may I help you this evening."

"I'd like a room, please."

"Would you like a suite or one of our fine single rooms?"

I think about it for a second. *"I'll take a suite, please ."*

"How many nights is your stay?"

"Two nights for now. I might need a third."

"That's fine. Just let us know when you decide."

I nod my head. He types on the keyboard. I feel as if someone is watching me. I tilt my head down and peek over my shoulder. A man quickly looks down at a clipboard in his hand. He uses the pen in his hand. It looks like he signed his name or something. He hands the clipboard back to an employee. He looks in my direction then turns his back to me and walks toward the casino hallway.

"That's four hundred and forty-five dollars. Will that be cash or credit card?"

"Oh, umm, credit." I dig into my purse and get

my wallet out. I slide my card to the clerk. I glance back over my shoulder towards the casino. The man is long gone.

I sign for the room and get the room key card. The clerk tells me I'm on the top floor. I thank him and go to the elevators. This is the most calm I've felt all day. I am looking forward to showering and getting something to eat. Who knows what the rest of the evening will hold for me. Maybe I'll venture down to the casino and play some slots. I have no rules tonight. I have no man to meet or be with. It's just me and my freedom.

I get into my suite and wow, it's spectacular. I mean I know suites are supposed to be top-notch, but damn, I didn't think it would be this big. The bedroom is on a floor of its own. I carry my luggage up the spiral staircase. I set it down at the foot of the bed, then jump on the king-sized bed. I spread my arms and legs out. I get this entire bed alone. All night. I will go to bed alone and wake up alone. No going to sleep next to a man only to wake to see he snuck out before the sun came up. I let out a puff of air. Who am I kidding, myself? I don't like sleeping alone anymore. I have grown accustomed to having a warm body next to me. I leap off the bed! Nope, I'm not thinking about the last three months. Not thinking about Malcolm, Hawk, or Warrick. I'm also not thinking about Kaiden, the guy I haven't met yet. I am here for me and nobody else. I start down the spiral staircase, my phone rings from inside my purse. I should probably answer it, but ignoring it sounds like a better option. Whoever it is can leave a voicemail message. I'll return the call whenever I damn well feel like it. By the time I'm on the bottom step it stops ringing. I smile. I feel like a rebel.

As I am leisurely walking around the suite, I hear my phone ring again. Don't care. I open the mini-refrigerator and see little bottles of liquor. I read the labels. They are nothing that I'd drink alone. I get an idea. I find the room's phone and look for hotel room service pamphlets. I find the number and dial it. I order two glasses of milk with ice and nothing else. Probably an odd request, but it is what it is. I have them bill my room. I wander around while I wait for the kitchen to bring it up. I go to the floor to ceiling windows and pull back the curtains. All I see are neon lights for what seems like it goes for miles. For all I know, maybe it does. I step away from the window. I notice there are sliding glass doors. I go over and open the blinds. I won't be going out onto the balcony. I am not one to like heights. Oh no, I like my feet on solid ground. Probably why I don't like flying that much.

I smile when there is a knock on the door. That's got to be room service with my milk. It's time to get this no rules, no men party started. I am ready to just be carefree tonight. Just me and my drinks. I have this entire suite to myself and if I get bored, there's a casino downstairs. Who knows maybe I'll just go to the lounge and see what is happening. The possibilities seem to be endless tonight.

I took a nice relaxing bath in the jacuzzi tub, sipping on my White Russian drink I made. By the time I got out, I had finished my drink. I put on the hotel's fluffy bathrobe and went to make another drink. I am feeling quite relaxed. The only thing that is bothering me is my phone. It will not stop ringing. I have come to the conclusion that it is probably Grams calling me. I am not touching it. Not even to turn off the ringer. I have no desire to listen to her bitching at me. I cannot deal with her silent auction today. I need at least one day to just forget that I am in over my head. I don't know how to put everything into perspective. I really really don't want to think about it for one damn day.

I take my drink with me upstairs. I have decided that I am going to venture out. Where I am going to go is unknown at this time. I guess that will be wherever my feet take me. I open my suitcase and take out a cocktail dress I brought with me. It's a cute little black dress. It isn't too revealing, but it is sexy enough to turn some heads. Not that I need to turn heads at this point. I need no man to come on to me. I have enough problems in that area as it is.

I slip the dress on, grab my makeup bag and go into the bathroom. I take my hair down from the clip I used to hold it up while bathing. I run my fingers through my dark locks. I have to admit, it doesn't look too shabby. I freshen up my makeup, having a few sips of my drink as I apply it. I lean in closer to the mirror when adding pink lip gloss. I stand back and check myself out. Not too bad, I think to myself. I think I am ready for a night out by myself. There is a little part of me that wishes Porter was with me. He would know what to do. I am kind of going at this blindly. I would never in a million years go out alone at home. I'm just not that type of person. I get my purse before going back down the spiral staircase, leaving my phone behind. As the old saying goes, here goes nothing.

When I get to the first floor, I decide to go into the lounge. I haven't eaten today so maybe I can grab a bite to eat. I have a seat at the bar. I order a drink when the male bartender comes over to me. I ask for a menu as well. I look at the appetizers. I am not super hungry, but if I am going to keep drinking tonight, I need a little something in my belly. Once I place my order, I take a look around. I notice the man from earlier at the end of the bar. I caught him looking at me and our eyes connected. He looks similar to Kaiden now that I see his face. I don't believe it's him, but he could pass as Kaiden. This man turns his head and looks at someone else. He doesn't glance back at me before leaving the lounge. I have to say, he is a very attractive man. He has this mysterious persona about him. I find it a little sexy.

I stay in the lounge long enough to nibble on some food. I feel a bit out of place. I pay my tab and leave. As I enter the main area, I read the neon light to Seven Jewels Casino. I might as well give it a shot. I have nothing to lose. Well except money. I have not gambled before, therefore, I have no idea what I am in for. I should probably set myself a limit. I don't really care to go broke in Vegas.

I wandered around for a while until I found a machine I wanted to try. I watched over the shoulder of other players trying to get a feel for what to do. It seems simple enough. I put a twenty in the machine and pick my bet. Before I know it, my money is gone. I haven't won a damn thing. How do people think this is fun? This is like tossing money out a window to never be seen again. It bugs me that I won nothing. So what do I do? I add more money. I keep hitting that button over and over. I'm such a dork when I win a dollar twenty.

"You are never going to win if you only bet thirty cents."

I look behind me and it's him. The handsome man from earlier. *"How much should I be betting?"*

"Max bet, baby. Go big or go home."

I roll my eyes, but damn me I increase my bet to the max. I hit that damn button and I am shocked when I won a bunch of free games. I turn to say something to the man but he is gone. I look around for him but he seems to have vanished into thin air. I cash out when my free games are done.

"Nice win!"

"Huh?"

"Your win, eleven hundred dollar win is nice."

I look at my printed ticket. I guess the girl sitting

next to me was right. *"Thanks. Did you see the man who was talking to me?"*

"How could I not."

"Do you know where he went?"

She points over her shoulder with her thumb. I say thanks and walk away in the opposite direction she told me he went in. I think it is time I call it a night. I glanced at the ticket in my hand, at least I won some money. Too bad I have no idea what to do with this ticket. I can figure that out tomorrow. I think it's best for me to retire to my suite for the night. I could use a good night of sleep.

CHAPTER TWO
CIARA

I slept great last night. I don't know what it was, but I hit the pillow and I was out. Very unusual for me when being in a new place. I have to assume the White Russians helped out a lot. Whatever the reason, I'll take it. I wasn't up half the night tossing and turning. Even better, I didn't think about Malcolm, Hawk or Warrick. It's not that I don't want to think about these guys, because they are such wonderful men. I do feel blessed to have met them. It all boils down to I have no idea who I love the most. Who I can see standing with me at the end of all this. I may be so messed up by the time I meet all these guys that I could possibly screw everything up. I could end up the way I started, alone. That scares me. I don't want to go through every emotion there is to just end up alone. All the men have told me they will be waiting for me to choose them. Seven more months is a long time to ask anyone to wait.

I got dressed in a pair of blue jeans and a light sweater. I came down to the Hotel's restaurant to have some breakfast and to return Grams thirty missed phone calls last night. I know she is going to ream my ass out for ignoring her calls. She is not going to be happy with me if I tell her I am in Nevada and not home. The way I see it, no difference between being here alone or home alone. So she shouldn't be mad, but she will be seeing things from her own point of view and not mine.

I get another coffee before calling her back. I make myself comfortable as well, this conversation will probably be a long one. I cross my fingers that she doesn't yell at me too much.

"Ciara Verbank, where in the world are you?"

"Las Vegas." I don't think that sunk in.

"I went to your apartment and called you over a dozen times last night. I have been worried sick about you."

"I am fine. I just needed a night to recoup."

"Are you home now? I am heading over to your place."

"Grams, I am in Las Vegas."

"You are what? Are you with Kaiden?"

"No, I am alone. I am at a sweet hotel. I did some gambling last night, had a few drinks and went to bed."

"Did you forget about your obligations yesterday?"

"What are you talking about?"

"Jacquelyn Sanders, does that ring a bell?"

Oh, shit! I sorta did forget about her. *"I'm not going to lie, I knew about it, then it slipped my mind."*

"This is to help you, Ciara. The tabloids are having a field day with you."

"I know. I'm sorry."

Her silence tells me she is thinking. *"I wish you thought about this before you took off. Why would you go there days before you were supposed to?"*

"I needed space. This isn't easy for me. I am trying my damndest to fulfill your damn auction. Grams, my emotions are fucked. I feel like I can't breathe."

"You didn't need to fly across the country for space. Don't you get that I am here for you? I am right here waiting for you to share your experience with me. I don't even know if you have had a connection with these men."

"That's the problem. I fucking love all three of them. You are right, I didn't need to fly across the

country to have space, but don't you get that you are sending me here anyways?"

"I really wish you would not swear, Ciara. How about I fly out and we can spend a few days together?" How do I tell the one person who has always had my back that I just want to be alone? *"I would really love to hear about your experience so far."*

"The men you picked are really wonderful men. They each have qualities you would want for me. I could see a happy, loving life with all three men I met so far. I love each one differently. I am trying to have a few days to sort things out. I would love to see you, Grams, I really would, but I kind of just want to chill here in Vegas alone. Please don't take that as I am dissing you. I am not doing that."

"I understand. Can you at least make time to speak with Jacquelyn, today?"

"Yes. Text me her information and I will contact her later."

"I love you, my sweet girl."

"I love you too, Grams."

That wasn't as bad as I thought it would be. I finish my coffee and leave some cash on the table for my bill. I gather up my belongings I brought down with me and leave the Hotel's restaurant. I am going to do some exploring today and just enjoy the day.

Who knows, fresh air might do me some good and I can get myself together. I feel good today, even after that phone call with Grams.

I walk the streets and take in the sights of the shops, casinos and the people. It is very weird to see so many people dressed in costumes out in the public. Tourists like myself stand out. Which seems to be no big deal to the ones who live and work here. It makes it easy for the workers to hand out flyers to the tourists. I have received quite a few today.

I have been walking around for hours. I found a cute little cafe and decided to go inside to get a drink. I get an orange juice smoothie and have a seat near the window where I can people watch. What catches my eye is the place across the street. I recognize it from the three-ring binder. I wasn't going to go there until I was supposed to meet Kaiden Marcellus. Now that I am this close, I am tempted to change my mind. What could it hurt if I just take a peek inside his place? I can pop in and get a feel for his environment then sneak right back out. He'll never know I invaded his space before we meet tomorrow. Honestly, I don't care if he finds out that I was there. What's he going to do about it, not date me. That would be a win for me in my opinion.

I cross the street and dump my drink in the trash. When I reach Vibe, I pull the door open. I step inside and even though it is mid-afternoon the place is busy. I take a seat at the bar. I don't see a bartender so I scan the dance club. There is a huge dance floor. I can see a DJ booth on the far wall and on either side of that is a spiral staircase that takes you up to a platform with metal railing. I will assume that is for dancers as well. I notice a staircase off to the left. I am unsure where that leads. It could very well be another floor for different music. I could be wrong. To the far right is a door. It reads private. That possibly could be an office, but again, I don't know for sure. I am just guessing.

"Hi, what can I get you to drink?"

"Oh, umm, I am here to see Kaiden Marcellus." Why did that just come out of my mouth?

"Let me go and see if he's available."

"Thanks."

I cannot believe I just said that. I could slap myself right now. I watch the girl go over to the door that reads private. I should get the hell out of here before he comes out from his office and sees me. For some goddamn reason, my ass is glued to this barstool. Maybe I am a glutton for punishment. I keep my attention on that door. I sit up a little straighter when I see a man and woman come out together. It shuts behind them. My shoulders slump when it isn't Kaiden. Then it opens again. The bartender waves me over. I get off the barstool. Great, now my ass isn't glued to it! When I reach the girl, she brings me through the door. It is dark in here. The only lighting is a dim red light. You can barely see ten feet in front of you. It gives me chills. It is a little creepy. We didn't go far. Thank God. We go into a room and she shuts the door behind us.

"What's your shirt size?"

"Excuse me?"

"Shirt size for your uniform. You are here for the waitress job, correct?"

I think I just found my way out of this mess. *"I wear a medium."*

"And bottoms?"

I look at her spandex short shorts. *"Medium."*

"Small it is." Why even ask me if you aren't going to listen? *"Kaiden told me to tell you to be here tonight by eight."*

"Oh, I am working tonight?"

"You are if you want the job."

I follow her back out into the dark hallway. She's

a friendly one. Glad I won't be working here for real. How unprofessional of Kaiden to not even come out to meet his potential new employee. Whatever, not my business. He can run it however he wishes. Not like I am going to show up to wait tables for him tonight anyway. I think I have seen enough. He just might be making this easy for me to not fall in love with him.

CHAPTER THREE
KAIDEN

It's damn near eight and my new hire hasn't shown up yet. Hiring someone is easy, getting them to show up for their shift is another story in itself. The thing that pisses me off is the girl was overly excited to work here when I gave her the job this morning. I told her to come back later in the day for her uniform and I would give her the time to start then. She showed up for the uniform, now where the hell is she? I am giving her five more minutes, if she shows up after that, I'm firing her. I don't tolerate tardiness. Especially on the first day. I am not a damn babysitter.

Jackie McCain comes into my office and lets me know my new hire showed. I relax a little. I tell her to show her the ropes and then let her go off on her own in about an hour. The girl said she waited tables before. Jackie leaves my office. Jackie is one of my main girls. She's been with me for years. I don't trust many, but I trust her. I sit back in my chair and turn the cameras to another feed. I have more than one business to run. I must keep my eye on both.

All seems to be running smoothly. Which is good as it makes my job easier. I push out from the desk and leave my office. I go to the right down the dark hallway. I enter my second business. The one I enjoy the most. I do a walkthrough before I go into the dressing room. Another employee of mine is here.

"Hey, Sara."

"Hello, Mr. Marcellus."

"What are you doing in here?"

"I forgot to put this on." She shows me her necklace.

Sara Gonzales has been with me for quite some time. She is very good at what she does and the clientele loves her. *"Do you need help putting that on?"*

"Nah, I am a pro by now. Thanks anyway."

I follow Sara out of the dressing room. She's been quiet lately. I sense something is off with her. I have a feeling what it is, but I am going to watch her in the next few days to see if I am right or not. If I am, I may have to let her go. She'll be breaking the contract and I can't have that. It's not good for business.

I sit at the bar and order a whiskey on the rocks. I have the best view of my place. I sit back and relax. Tonight is busier than normal for a Thursday. Weekends tend to be the hot nights. I'll take whatever revenue these people want to give me. I like money! I like having a shit ton of it. The more I have, the earlier I can retire and enjoy life as it passes by. I don't want to live in Vegas my entire life. I could retire now if I wanted, but I plan on doing this a few more years. I am not ready to give up the club life just yet. I like the mixture of people who come through my doors.

I hung out long enough. Looks like Sara and I will have to have a talk tomorrow. I am hoping I am seeing something that isn't there. As I said she's one of my top girls. I am not going to worry about tonight. I have a club that needs my attention right now.

I walk through the door and enter the nightclub. The lights are dimmed and the dance floor is jammin. I like it. Vibe is one hell of a place to hang out. I built this place almost ten years ago. It was a shit hole when I bought it. I did a lot of renovation before I opened the doors. Ever since then, it's the place to be if you want great drinks and good music. I have two floors. The music is different on the floors. When you own a club you have a lot of different people to satisfy. I take pride in giving the people what they want. Not only did I choose to have two floors, but I also have a drink specialist. He is one hell of a mixer. Vibe has its own line of alcoholic drinks because of him. I put my heart and soul into this place. There was no option to fail. So, seeing my club full makes me excited. The more drinks that are poured, the more money I make.

I grab Jackie as she passes by me. *"Where is the new hire?"*

"I am letting her be on her own. You said I only needed to be with her an hour."

"You did make sure she was ready before you did that, correct?"

"Yes, Mr. Marcellus. She seemed fine."

I nod and move on. I need to find this girl to make sure she really is fine. Tonight is busier than I anticipated. I wouldn't normally start a new girl under these circumstances. I don't want to scare any new girl off on their first night due to being overwhelmed.

I stand near the dance floor, scouting the crowd for the new girl. I look for every blonde headed woman here. I don't see her. I turn and face the bar in case I missed her getting drinks. I laugh inside. I have a new girl, but not the one who is supposed to be working. *"Poor girl has no idea what she has done,"* I say under my breath. Jackie passes by me again. *"Jackie, is that the new hire?"* I point to Ciara over her shoulder.

She glances over her shoulder. *"Yep, that's the one."*

"She's not the new hire."

"It's who you told me to give the uniform to."

I wave Jackie off with my hand. I guess this is what I get for not doing things myself. I can't be mad at Jackie, it's not her fault. However, Ciara is a different story. I need to find out why she is portraying herself as a waitress and didn't tell Jackie she wasn't here for a job. Why the hell is she here anyway? I was supposed to pick her up tomorrow. I smile, someone doesn't like to play by the rules. My palms tingle. This whole dating Ciara for a month just got more exciting. I'm going to have fun with this.

I walk up behind Ciara and I grab her elbow. Hmm, I like the sound of a gasp leaving her throat. *"Put the tray down and follow me."* I wave my bartender over. *"Make sure these drinks get where they belong."*

I walk away with Ciara's arm in my hand. *"Let go of me."*

I don't listen. I keep going to the private area. I bring her into the dressing room. *"What do you think you are doing?"*

"What did it look like? I was waiting on people who want drinks."

I laugh. She wants to play this off as if I don't know who she is. Game on, baby. I can assure her, I am better at this than she is. *"You are in the wrong club, sweetheart. Therefore you are also in the wrong uniform."*

I hand her a little something else to put on. And I mean, little. Her eyes get big when she sees there isn't much to her outfit. I walk over to the locked safe and open it. *"What are you waiting for? Get changed."*

"You are crazy, I am not putting this on."

"Don't you want to see what is behind door number two?"

She swallows. *"Turn around."*

I go back to the safe and get out a necklace for my new hire. Damn, I can't wait to show her door number two. I wasn't going to at all, but Ciara changed the game, I guess I can too. I was going to keep this part of me a secret until I knew the girl, but this is so much better.

"Are you changed?"

"I am damn well about naked."

I walk up to Ciara. Damn, she is sexy. I step around her heated body and stop behind her. I put the necklace around her throat. It's not really a necklace at all. It's a choker. This is how my clientele know these are my girls. They are to keep their hands off. I move around to the front of her and look at my handy work. Ciara touches the choker. *"Stunning."* I take her hand and pull her out of the dressing room. I take her down the dark hallway to another door. I smile, I cannot wait for her reaction. I press my hand to the keypad and the door unlocks.

We step inside and I lead her to the bar. I pull out a barstool for her and she sits down. Her eyes are wide open when she gets her first look at the real Vibe. I see something right away that I don't like. *"Don't move. I'll be right back."*

I walk fiercely across the room. I reach the corner booth where Sara is getting a shot licked off her chest. That is fine, that is not breaking rules. It's where the client's hand is that is breaking my rules. *"Get your fucking hands off my girl. You know better."* Sara leaps from the table. She knows I am pissed. She crossed a line. A line she knew not to ever cross. *"Go, home. We will talk tomorrow,"* I tell Sara. I look at

Mr. Watson. *"You know the rules. Do you want your membership canceled?"*

"No, sir, I don't."

"I suggest you call it a night. Don't ever touch my girls again. You got me?" He nods his head.

I am fucking pissed. You want to stay on my good side, don't break my rules. It is as simple as that. I have no problem putting anyone in their place. I turn around and Ciara's eyes are glued on me. I walk back over to where she is. She tries to break eye contact with me.

"Seen enough, Ms. Verbank?"

"Yes," she whispers.

We get out in the hallway. I pin her body to the wall. *"What are you doing here? I was supposed to pick you up tomorrow."*

"I came early. I came here today to meet you and I was given a uniform. I thought I could see into your life before we met."

"You see that was a mistake, right?"

"Yes."

"Where are you staying?"

"Seven Jewels."

I let out a puff of air. That makes my blood boil. *"I guess I'll have someone go and pack up your things."*

"I can pack my own things."

"Not anymore you can't. You broke the rules, so I am going to fix them." I step away from Ciara. *"Let's go."*

"Where are we going?"

"Home, right after you change your clothes."

CHAPTER FOUR
CIARA

What the everloving hell was I thinking? Better yet, who the hell is Kaiden Marcellus? If Grams saw what I just saw, I don't think his bid to date me would have flown. If she visited Vibe before, I don't think she ever saw what is behind door number two, that's for sure. What I witnessed would be enough to knock her socks off.

I change my clothes and my heart is beating faster than it ever has before. On top of what unfolded behind the second door, I think Kaiden is pissed at his employees and me as well. Technically, he has no right to be pissed at me. He's the one that didn't come out from the office to see who wanted to speak to him. It was him that had that girl give me a uniform. I just went along with it.

Kaiden's demeanor seems a little calmer when he asks if I am ready to go. I don't answer him, I just give him a head nod. He doesn't say anything back to me either. He leaves the dressing room and I follow him out. He doesn't say goodbye to anyone, he just walks out the front entrance. He opens a car door for me and I get in. I buckle my seatbelt as I watch him walk around the front of the car. He gets in and starts the car. I am jolted back into the seat as he takes off. He shifts gear before I can look out the back window to see if he cut someone off or if there was no traffic. I don't even think he looked before taking off. I am beginning to think Grams has no idea who this man is.

"Where are you taking me?"

"My place."

"I want to go back to the hotel I'm staying at."

"Not going to happen."

"You can't make me come with you."

"I didn't make you get in my car."

"I want out."

Kaiden ignores my comment. He continues to speed through the streets. He weaves through traffic as if he's in a damn race. I'm over here with my foot pressed into the floorboard of this car, wishing I had a brake pedal. I dated a race car driver who drove faster, but yet, I felt safer. Even Pat didn't scare me this much.

Kaiden slams on the brakes for a red light. I whip my door open and get my seatbelt off. I am out of that car before he can stop me and run to the sidewalk. I'm not getting back in that car with him. I begin to walk the sidewalk. I hear the tires peel out on the pavement. I move further away from the road. I walk as close to the buildings as I can.

Kaiden drives slow with the window down. *"Ciara, get back in the car. You do not want to be in this part of town alone at this hour."*

"Not a chance, asshole."

I walk a little faster. Fuck him. I see him out of the corner of my eye still tagging along from his sports car. I suddenly turn around and walk back the way we just came. See how he likes that. Can't follow me now can he!? I shut my eyes briefly. Seriously, he is going to drive in reverse now! This guy is unbelievable. Although I gotta say, he's making it very easy for me to not like him at all. His head is so big, he probably doesn't even realize what an ass he is. He's got to be the most arrogant person I have ever met.

I scream when Kaiden comes up from behind me and grabs me. I try to elbow him in the stomach but my arms are pinned to my sides. His hand covers my mouth when I scream again. His hold on me loosens because of it and I elbow him. I wiggle as my feet are lifted off the ground. I wiggle and fight to be released. I hear tires squeal. I continue to kick and scream. Suddenly I am falling backward, landing on top of a body. I hear Kaiden say, *"Let go of her."* I am freed and I get to my feet. I should run away but I look to see what the hell is happening. Kaiden has some man in a chokehold. Through heavy breathing, he tells me to get in the car. I can't just leave him fighting off my attacker. I watch as they roll around on the ground. Kaiden punches the guy who attacked me. Then the guy gets free after Kaiden gets to his feet. The guy runs off. Kaiden looks at me as he straightens his suit jacket. I stare at him like a deer caught in headlights. Everything happened so fast. He comes toward me like a lion going after his prey. I step back.

"Are you okay? Did you get hurt?"

"I think I am fine. Your lip is bleeding."

He uses the top of his hand to touch his lip. He looks at the blood spot. *"Let's get you out of here."*

We start to head back to his car, that's when it happens. The squealing of tires echoes in the empty street. His car just got hijacked and it's all my fault. I cover my face with my hands to hide. I am ashamed of myself. I didn't listen when he said this neighborhood isn't good. I wish I could go back and start this entire day over. I would think twice about going to Vibe to meet Kaiden before I was supposed to.

Kaiden gets his phone from the inside pocket of his suit jacket. I listen as he calls someone he knows to come and get us. When he hangs up I ask him if he is going to call the police.

"Are you hurt?"

"No."

"Then no reason to call the police."

"What about your car?"

"My main concern right now is getting you the hell out of here. This is no place to be hanging out. Besides, it's just a fucking car."

A man that goes by the name of Bounce came and picked us up. He dropped us off in an extravagant neighborhood. Kaiden's home is beautiful from the gated driveway all the way to his home. It is dark outside but he has lawn lights that give off enough light to show he lives a comfortable life. This man has a lot of money.

"How much did you bid to date me?" I really

wish my mouth would shut up. I didn't mean for my thoughts to be voiced.

"Five hundred thousand dollars."

I swallow hard. Wow! *"Why on earth would you pay that much money to date me for a month?"*

"Because I am bored."

"What do you mean you are bored?"

"It means I am tired of dating women who come into Vibe just to meet me. They are all the same."

"Hmm."

"It's not the only reason."

"What is the other reason?"

"I happen to like Millie's charity."

"Oh."

"Do you want to sit out here all night or would you rather go inside? Personally, I could use a drink."

Kaiden thanks Bounce for the ride. We get out of the car and walk up to the front stoop. Kaiden opens the door and I step in first. His home is very big. He puts a hand to my lower back and we go into a room. He offers for me to sit at his home bar. He goes behind it and asks what I would like to drink. I told him to surprise me. He puts two shot glasses on the bartop and pours two shots. He then slides one over to me. I take it up and slam it.

"Damn, what was that?" I wipe my eyes that are watering from the burn.

"Something my mixologist mixed up. Good, right?"

"Oh it's good, but it's hot."

He pours us another one. Then he pours two glasses of something else. He comes around from behind the bar and sits next to me. He then takes the two shots and hands me one of them. We drink them. His eyes travel to my knee. My jeans are ripped and my knee was bleeding.

"Come with me."

"Where are we going?"

"Upstairs."

We take the grand staircase up to the second floor. He leads me into a bedroom and then into the master bath. He starts the water in the tub. What the hell is he doing? He leaves the bathroom and comes back with a t-shirt. He tells me he'll be back in a while. He wants me to take a bath? This man is confusing. I don't know at this point if he's a jerk or a nice guy hiding behind this dominating force. He shuts the door behind him when he leaves me to bathe. I strip out of my clothes and get into the bath. I lean back and relax. This day has been different, but this evening has been an enigma.

CHAPTER FIVE
KAIDEN

Meeting Ciara hasn't gone as planned. For one, the girl wasn't supposed to show up at Vibe unannounced. I was supposed to pick her up tomorrow from the airport. I had the entire day all planned out. Shopping, dinner, and then show her some of Vegas before taking her to my home. I wanted to give her a good impression of me. Instead, I give her a shit-show. The evening has been worse than a train wreck. Fucking Christ, I blindly hired the girl to work for me. She witnessed me losing my shit on a client and she saw my private club. The club that I wasn't going to show her right away, if at all. To top it all off, I almost get the girl mugged. It probably would have been way worse if I weren't there. Not the day I was expecting at all. Today was supposed to be about work and getting ready to take a few days off.

When I saw that Ciara's knee had bled. I felt horrible about her getting hurt. She was in my care and I allowed some asshole to put his hands on her. Because of me, I put her in harm's way. That angers me. For as long as she is with me, I won't allow that to happen again. She can fight all she wants against me, I will win that battle. Even if I have to pick her ass up and put her in my car or whatever if the situation arises again.

I left Ciara to bathe. I needed a minute to regroup. I take my suit jacket off and unbutton my button-down shirt. I leave my bedroom so that I can call the cops to report my car stolen. I almost don't want to bother with it. I was getting ready to trade it in any way. But that isn't who I am. You do wrong, you need to pay the consequences. A lesson I learned a long time ago the hard way.

I sat at my home bar and set my phone on the bartop. I pick up the drink I left sitting here when I took Ciara upstairs. I have one sip of my drink and my phone rings. I look at the screen and it's a private number. I answer it even though I normally wouldn't if the number is unknown.

"Hello."

"Hello, this the police department and I am calling because a car registered in your name has been involved in a motor vehicle accident."

"Christ. I was just about to call you and report it stolen. How bad is my car?"

"It's probably totaled. I am going to need some information from you."

After a half an hour or longer on the phone, we hang up. Looks like I am going to need a new car. I'm not heartbroken over the car. As I said I was going to trade it in anyway. This is just a headache I don't need or want. But, it is what it is. I am not going to dwell on it.

My attention goes to Ciara when she walks into the bar room I have set up at my house. She wears my t-shirt and I find that sexy as hell. She has a seat at the bar next to me. I slide her drink over in front of her.

"Feel better?"

"Yes, thank you."

I glance at her scraped up knee. *"I'll be right back."*

I run upstairs to my bathroom and get the first aid kit. I know she washed her knee, but I need to make sure the cuts heal. When I return, her eyes can't help but go to my chest. I get out the antibacterial cream and rub some on her knee.

"I don't think that's really necessary."

"You're probably right, but let's be cautious." I put a band aid over the cuts. *"My car was found."*

"Oh, good."

"It's totaled."

"Ohhh."

I lean back on the barstool. There's an awkward silence between us. She quietly sips on her drink and I silently watch her. Ciara is a gorgeous woman. She first caught my attention in New York when I saw her at a fashion show. I was there with an old friend of mine who was modeling for Ciara's clothing line. I didn't meet Ciara but I saw her from across the room. I did however meet Millie. I was surprised when she contacted me about her silent auction. I am bored, I didn't lie about that. I do like Millie's charity as well. What really made me do this was the simple fact that it was Ciara and I'd get to be with her for a month. I couldn't pass up such an opportunity. I had to know why a beautiful woman like Ciara is alone. Is she overworked? Does her beauty not match the personality? DId she not want to date? There could be so many reasons.

"When can I get my stuff from Seven Jewels?"

"I'll make arrangements for your things to be delivered here tomorrow."

"Why are you hellbent on not allowing me to get my own things?"

"Do you know who owns that place?"

"Nope, not a clue."

"I know the owner and let's just say we see things differently."

"What does that have to do with me?"

"You are breaking the rules your grandmother set."

"I really don't know what you are talking about."

"Want another drink?"

"No, thanks."

"Are you hungry?"

"I'm fine. I'm actually really tired. I think I'll retire for the night if you show me to my room."

"Of course."

I show Ciara to her room. I put her in the guest bedroom down the hall from me. I don't know if I am relieved she wanted to go to bed or disappointed. I can't blame her for being tired. This evening hasn't exactly been a walk in the park. Being attacked has got to be physically and emotionally exhausting. I hope that's her reason for going to bed. I would be frustrated if I knew it were just to get away from me.

"Goodnight."

"Goodnight."

I don't bother to go back downstairs. I go to my room instead. I take my shirt off and toss it in the laundry bin. I then sit at the foot of my bed to take my shoes and socks off. I stand and remove my pants. I drop them in the laundry bin on the way to the bathroom. I check my lip out in the mirror. I bit it as we all fell to the ground when I grabbed Ciara's attacker from behind. It's only a tiny cut. Not a big deal.

I am pretty exhausted myself. I don't usually get to bed this early. I keep club hours. Since I rarely get any sleep I might as well take advantage of being home at this hour. I slip into bed. Before I turn out the light, I send Sara a text to meet me at ten a.m. at Vibe. Then I send a text to Jackie to see how things are going. I'm really not used to being away from the clubs.

I am reading Jackie's reply that everything is good when Ciara comes tiptoeing into my room. I peek at her as if I didn't notice her. I type a reply to Jackie. The covers get pulled back on the opposite side of the bed and Ciara crawls in underneath the blanket. What the hell is she doing? She makes herself comfortable on her side, facing away from me. I guess she's sleeping in my bed! Women don't sleep in my bed. Not once has a woman ever even slept in my house, let alone my bed.

I put my phone on the night stand and turn the light off. I scoot down in the bed to put my head on my pillow. I bring my arms up and latch my fingers behind my head. I stare up at the dark ceiling. It might take me all night to fall asleep. I feel the mattress move, next thing I know, Ciara's body is snuggling up to mine. Now I'm really awake and so is my manhood. So much for getting extra sleep tonight.

CHAPTER SIX
CIARA

I put my jeans on that I wore yesterday, then I ventured out of Kaiden's bedroom. I didn't last long in his guest bedroom. I went into his room last night after I couldn't stop tossing and turning. Granted I only stayed in that bedroom for about fifteen minutes, I knew I wasn't going to be able to sleep alone. New house, a new guy, and being attacked didn't help at all. All I could feel was that man's arms wrapped around my body. I shouldn't have gotten out of Kaiden's car. I should have listened when he said it wasn't a safe neighborhood. But no, I let my emotions cloud my judgment. Anyway, there was no way I was going to get any sleep being alone. Kaiden didn't seem to mind me crashing in his bed. If he did, he didn't say anything about it to me.

I find Kaiden in his kitchen after searching for

him. It took a minute since I don't know his house because he didn't bother giving me a tour. I'm not upset about that. I understand last night was a clusterfuck. I am hoping today will be better. We definitely got off on the wrong foot. I know I am particularly to blame. I should have never gone to Vibe dressed as one of his waitresses. I should have gone as myself or not at all. I can't take all the blame, he didn't need to be a dick when he realized who I was. Laugh it off as I was planning on doing.

"Good morning, Kaiden."

"Morning, Ciara. I was just about to come up and wake you. I have breakfast ready in the dining room."

I take a glimpse around. He's the only one here beside me. *"You made me breakfast?"*

"I did. I wasn't sure what you would like so I picked a few different things. It's on the table."

We go into the dining room and see the display of food. A few things? He damn near put the entire kitchen in here. There's so much fresh fruit cut up. There's also waffles, bacon, sausage, egg whites, and English muffins. How in the world does he think two people are going to eat all this food? What is it with men having so much food to eat?

We sit at the table and Kaiden waits for me to start picking what I want to eat. I get a waffle and some fruit. He gets an English muffin and builds himself a breakfast sandwich. I watch him take a little bit of each piece of fruit. What we took didn't even put a dent in the amount of food he prepared.

"Did you sleep well?"

"I slept pretty well."

"How about you?"

"I got enough sleep." He takes a bite of his sandwich. *"We have a busy day today. I'm looking forward to having a fresh start to our relationship."*

"Me too." I am relieved that he said that. I would love to put yesterday behind us. *"Are my things here?"*

"You will have your belongings soon. After we eat, we will be leaving."

Why do I feel like I should say yes sir to him? I don't think Kaiden is a laid back mellow kind of guy. I see him as having everything planned out from the time he wakes in the morning to the time he goes to bed at night. Holy hell if things don't go his way. I get having a plan, but I believe he might need to chill out a bit. I am hoping I am reading him all wrong.

"So, I am wearing yesterday's clothes?"

"Until we go out, yes."

I eat my breakfast to keep my mouth from telling him to shove it. He is making it very easy for me to not fall in love with him. I mean, seriously what is his deal? Is he a control freak or something? I don't get his deal with me not being able to get my own things from the hotel last night. It doesn't make any sense at all to me. I would have clean clothes to wear today if he stopped at the hotel last night. I wouldn't have had to wear his shirt to bed either.

He looks at his phone and then looks at me. His eyes are telling me he read something he didn't like. He replies to whoever texted him. I continue to eat. I'm not going to ask what just happened. He gets another message, looks at it, then places the phone on the table. *"You didn't tell me you have a dog!"*

I swallow the food in my mouth. I am a horrible person. How on earth could I forget about Alaska? I hope my puppy is okay. I could burst into tears right now. *"If you would have taken me to my hotel suite you would have known."* I feel even worse putting the blame on him. *"Is that a problem?"*

"That you have a dog? Not really. I would have sent someone sooner if I had known."

"Someone is in my room right now? Is Alaska alright?"

"Your dog is fine."

"When can I get my dog back?"

"After you finish eating we are leaving."

I am not even hungry anymore. I push my food around with my fork, getting lost in thoughts. I am worried about my pup. I am so ashamed of myself. How could I be so thoughtless? I really am losing mind, aren't I? I would never do something like this if I were in the right state of mind.

"I'm done eating. Can I be excused? I have something I need to do."

"You barely touched your food. Are you alright?"

"Yes, there's something that I really need to do."

I get up from the table and go running from the room. I find my way upstairs to the guest room and lock the door behind me. I go right for my cell phone. I take a deep breath and call Malcolm. Tears start to flow before he even answers.

"Hey, babe. I didn't think I would hear from you today."

Through tears, I say, *"I am so sorry, Malcolm."*

"For what?"

"I need you to do me a big favor. If you can't do it, I understand."

"What do you need?"

"I need you to come to Vegas and get Alaska. I need you to keep her for me until this shit is over with."

"Wow. Did something happen?" I can't even

answer him as I cry harder. *"Ciara, what's going on?"*

"I was attacked last night and I left her in a hotel room all night alone."

"What!? What do you mean attacked?"

"I'm fine. Kaiden scared him off. I went to his house with him instead of going back to the hotel. I am so ashamed of myself."

"I think you have a reasonable excuse, so don't worry about it. Did you get hurt?"

"I'm fine, just a little scrape on my knee. Can you come and get her? If not I can ask Porter."

"Ciara, I wish I could. I am out of the country until next week."

"Okay. I'll ask Porter."

There is a bit of awkward silence. I try to wipe the tears from my eyes. I hear a knock on the bedroom door. *"I have to go."*

"Don't hang up. If Porter can't come and get her, I will find a way to do it myself."

Kaiden knocks again. *"I really need to go."*

"I am worried about you. You don't sound like yourself."

"I'm fine. I really have to go."

"I love you."

"I know." I hang up before he can say anything else.

I wipe my eyes again and go to unlock the bedroom door. When I opened it, Kaiden was walking away. *"I'll be ready in a minute. I am trying to get a hold of my friend Porter to see if he can come and get Alaska."*

"You don't have to send your dog home."

"Yeah, I kinda do. I'm not sending her, I am seeing if he can come to get her."

"You want your friend to come here?"

"Yeah, is that alright with you?"

"Let me know if he does, I'll pay for the ticket. I don't want you to send your dog away because of one night."

"I know."

"How long do you need? I have a car waiting for us."

I could call him from the car if you don't care that I am on the phone."

"Not at all."

Kaiden had a full-size SUV in the driveway waiting for us. We had to drop the driver off then he drove us through Sin City. I called Porter and my spirits lifted when he said he'd come to get Alaska. I booked him a flight using Kaiden's credit card. I tried paying for it myself, but he insisted on paying. Porter's flight leaves in a couple of hours, and honestly, I cannot wait to see him. I want to put my arms around my friend and hug him tight. I really miss him. I haven't seen him since Warrick took him out to dinner with us. I miss a lot about my life. I would love to sit down and design a new dress or outfit. By the time the next seven months go by, I sure hope I don't forget how to sew.

We pull up out front of Vibe and the place looks so much different to me in the daytime. I get out and so does Kaiden. He puts his hand to my lower back as we walk toward the front entrance.

"I have something I need to attend to, then we can get our day started."

"Okay."

"I think you are going to like what awaits you inside."

I smile even though I have no idea why I am smiling. We go to the bar and he tells me to have a seat.

He then calls a girl, Jackie, over to us. I cringe when I see it is the same girl who gave me the uniform.

"Jackie, meet Ciara. Ciara, this is Jackie. She's one of my best employees."

We say hi and then she says, *"I think I have something that belongs to you."*

I watch her go to the other end of the bar. I hadn't noticed the girl sitting there when we came in. Now that I have, I see it is the girl from door number two. I get a huge smile when I see my puppy. Thank god she's in one piece. Jackie hands her to me and I hug my baby. I kiss her and tell her how sorry I am.

"Thank you, Jackie."

"You bet."

"I need a few minutes, then we can go."

"Okay."

I don't even care what he's about to do. I am happy just having Alaska back with me. I am sad that I am sending her home, but I know it's just getting too difficult to give her the attention she needs right now. I kinda wish I left her with Shay. Shay gave her so much love. *"You would have liked that, huh, Alaska?"*

CHAPTER SEVEN
KAIDEN

Seeing Ciara with her puppy I think it's the first time I have seen her really smile. It's the same smile she had when I first saw her across the room in New York. I want to be the reason she smiles like that. I want to be the one that makes her laugh and be happy. It's why I signed up for this. I walk away from the girl who makes my heart skip a few beats to deal with Sara. I can't wait to get this over with so that I can spend the day getting to know Ciara.

I sit down at the bar next to Sara. She doesn't even bother to look at me. *"Good morning."*

"Good morning, Mr. Marcellus."

"Care to explain to me what happened last night?"

"Not really. You pretty much saw what was going on."

"Are you and Mr. Watson in a relationship?"

"Yes."

"I figured as much. You have been with me for a long time. You know that I play by the rules I set. I place these rules to protect you girls. You know that when your choker is on, you are off-limits to the men touching you. I can't have one of my girls breaking rules."

"I know."

"Sara, look at me." She lifts her head and makes eye contact for the first time since me sitting next to her. *"Your happiness means the world to me. If you find that you want to be with Mr. Watson I am not going to stop you. What you do inside these walls is my business, though. I can't protect you or the other girls if you break the contract. How long has this been going on?"*

"Only a couple of months."

I scratch the back of my head. There are guidelines I put in place for my girls. I had to do that to make my private club a success and different from the rest on the strip. *"I have a question for you. Do you want out of your contract?"*

"Mr. Marcellus, working for you has been a great pleasure. With that said, I can't deny that I fell in love and I want to be with Mark."

"Mr. Watson is still a member. I guess I will see you around from time to time as a customer instead of an employee. I wish you the best."

"Just like that, you are letting me break the contract and still allowing Mark his membership?"

"You need the rooms, don't you?" I get up from the barstool. *"Be happy, Sara and don't be a stranger."* I wink at her and smile before walking away.

I walk up behind Ciara and put a hand on her shoulder. *"Cute pup."* There's the smile again that attracted me to her.

"Thanks."

"Ready to spend the day together?"

"I am."

I brought Ciara shopping to one of the finest boutiques in Vegas. It was one of Millie's rules. She is in the dressing room trying on dresses. I sit here on a red velvet loveseat waiting to see what she has picked out. I told her she is going to need a variety of clothing. She won't be needing the clothing she brought with her. She frowned on that, but she will get over it when she has more clothing than she can imagine. I told Ciara she is going to need dresses for evenings out and the rest is up to her.

I perk up when she comes out of the dressing room in a cocktail dress that is beautiful on her. She does a little swirl for me and I give her my approval. The next few dresses don't do it for me. She gives me an eye roll when I give the thumbs down each time. When she emerges in a dress laughing. I laugh too. She thinks she's being cute. She is, but this dress doesn't do it for me. I get up from the loveseat and walk over to where she stands a few feet away.

"Are you trying to be your grandmother?" She sticks out her tongue and then laughs. She is turning me on with that tongue of hers. She stops laughing when I back her back into the dressing room. She gasps when the door slammed shut behind me. I put my hands up on the wall to cage her in-between. I then run my fingertips along her jaw. I look her dead in the eyes. *"If I wanted to date a grandmother, I would have dated yours."* I wink to show her I can be playful too. *"Stick your tongue out at me again, I might give you something to lick."* I like the sound when she gasps again. I reach behind me and grab a hanger. I don't even look to see what it is. I hand it to her. *"Try this one on."* I step out of the dressing room. My manhood is wanting me to

go back in there and help her out of the dress she had on.

I pace the floor as Ciara changes into a different dress. I stop dead in my tracks when she comes out. She turns and puts her back to me and moves her dark thick hair out of the way. I step forward and zip the dress up. She peeks over her shoulder and thanks me. Damn, that's sexy. I want to pull her body back to me when she steps away.

"What do you think?"

"Absolutely stunning."

"Really?" I nod my head. *"You're not just saying that?"*

"Why would I lie?"

"Because it's one of my own dresses."

"I had no way of knowing that, Ms. Verbank."

She sticks her tongue out at me again and laughs. I warned her. I am a man of my word. I take her hand and bring her into the dressing room with me. I reach behind her to unzip the dress. She bites her lower lip as she blinks her eyes shut. I put my fingertips to her jaw and run them along the length until I reach her chin. I lift her face and press my lips to her. I give her a reason to use her tongue as it moves with mine. This woman makes me want to do all kinds of pleasurable things to her body. I want to rip her clothes off, bend her over my lap, and spank her delicious ass for starters. I want to show her just how much I want to introduce her to my world.

I step away from her. Her hand comes up to her lips. I give her a stare of lust. I want this woman more than I did before. My cock does too as it's hard as fuck in my pants. I grab her wrist and bring her hand from her lips to my manhood. I inch my way closer to her and lean down to her ear

"You make me so hard. I want to lick every inch of your body." With that said, I leave the dressing room. There's a proper place and time for me to devour her.

Shopping is done, thank god! I didn't know how much more my manhood could take from Ciara's teasing. After I kissed her, it seemed she purposely flaunted her body in front of me. I would say it was intentional. I am pleased this day is going much smoother than yesterday. I keep catching her looking at me from the corner of her eye as I drive us through Sin City. All my mind can think about is just how much sinful pleasure I want to unleash on her. I can't rush this, though. I need for her to like me before I show her the world I live in. The world I was going to keep from her completely or wait until later. I don't think I can withhold the truth of who I am. It's not the type of person I am.

"It's about that time to pick up your friend from the airport. I was thinking we could go back to my place, have a drink then go out to dinner."

"Porter would love that."

"How about you? Would you love that?"

She smiles. *"I would."*

"There's a really nice place I'd like to take you to dinner at. It would require you to wear that sexy dress you made."

"I think I can manage that."

"I look forward to this evening, Ms. Verbank."

She smiles. *"As do I."* Was there a hint of flirting in her voice?

I am not really excited for her friend to be with us tonight, but that's only because I want Ciara all to myself. Call me selfish, a dick or whatever else comes to mind. It doesn't bother me. A month isn't really all that long of a time. I need every minute of this time with her to see if this could be love.

CHAPTER EIGHT
CIARA

This day has gone by so fast. Shopping took up most of it. I wasn't thrilled to be trying on new clothes that I didn't necessarily need. However, I have to admit, I had a lot of fun. I got to see Kaiden relax a little which was really nice. I also got to see his playful flirty side. And boy, I gotta say, he had me wanting him. I feel there is something to this man that I haven't experienced before. Thinking about it makes my girly parts take notice. It also makes me a bit nervous. If he's into what I think he's into, I'm not sure I can be who he wants me to be. I'm not positive that I have it in my personality. That doesn't mean I'm not willing to give it a shot. There is this part of me that is very curious if I am right or not. When I think about Kaiden tying me up, my girly parts tingle, my thighs tighten, and my breathing changes. I just want him to take charge so that I can find out what that lifestyle is all about. I am pretty confident Kaiden wants to control me.

"Earth to Ciara." I snap out of my thoughts and I know I was caught daydreaming. *"Boy what I wouldn't give to know what's running through your thoughts right now."*

I laugh at Porter. *"A girl never tells her deepest secrets."*

Porter rolls his eyes. *"I need superpowers to be around you. You always leave out the juicy stuff."*

"Maybe the good stuff is too much information!" I laugh when he lets out a huff. *"Thank you so much for coming out here. Are you going to be okay taking care of Alaska?"*

He puts his hand up. *"I need a second to adjust my brain!"* I laugh and fall back on the bed. Porter and I are supposed to be getting ready to go to dinner. *"Okay. Off the non-sex talk to talk about your puppy. That's a one-eighty but I think I'm there. You know I gotcha, I would do anything for my girl."*

"You're the bestest."

"We better get ready. I don't see Kaiden as a man who likes to be late."

"Ya, he seems dominant."

"Mmmhmm. Yummy!"

I slap Porter's arm. *"You're bad!"*

"But oh so much fun."

"I'm so glad you are staying the night."

I get off the bed and Porter smacks my ass. I yelp. He jokes that I liked it. I leave his room and go down the hall to mine to get changed.

I put my hair up into a bun, pulling out a few strands to hang freely around my face. I already did my makeup before I went to check on Porter. I go out to the bedroom from the bathroom. All I have left to do is put my dress on. I go over to the closet and take my dress from the hanger and lay it on the bed. I drop my bathrobe to the floor, then my bra. I slip the dress on. I could do up the zipper myself, but I don't want to. I go over to the door and peek out into the hallway. I leave the guest bedroom and go to Kaidens room. I knock on the door frame and his attention turns to me. Kaiden is a beautiful man. He is tall and has dark hair. He keeps a beard trimmed close to his face. It's his piercing eyes that get me. They are dark brown and mysterious. I walked into his room and shut the door behind me. I go to stand before him and put my back to him. I hold my breath when his knuckles trace my spine. I stiffen when his fingers graze my skin as his hands slip into the front of my dress. He pinches my nipples.

"The things I want to do to your body makes me hard just thinking about it." I let out the breath I was holding. His hands leave my breasts and I whimper when he zips my dress. I want his hands back on me. He comes around to the front of me. *"Even more stunning than earlier."* His eyes travel to my mouth. My tongue darts out and I lick my lips. Damn it, I want him to kiss me the way he did this afternoon. I am not supposed to want him. I am not supposed to want Kaiden Marcellus to like me, either. *"We better get going before we are late."*

Kaiden moves away from me. I grab his wrist when he heads toward the door. I turn my head to look at him. What am I doing? Why am I giving him all the signs that I want him? His stare is something I haven't seen before. Kiss me damn it, I try telling him with my eyes. He doesn't say a word. He doesn't try to kiss me. I don't know what else to do, so I lace my fingers with his.

"Thank you for today." He winks at me and I smile, even though I can't help but feel disappointed he didn't kiss me.

We had a lovely dinner at Paza. It is a five star restaurant that Kaiden took me and Porter to. The food was outstanding and we had a couple of bottles of wine. The evening was very pleasant. The part I liked most was that Kaiden and Porter got along well together. I told Porter about Vibe and he wanted to see Kaiden's club. We finished the glasses of wine we all had then went to Vibe. When we got there, it was easy to slip into the environment. The music was blasting, the dance floor was inviting and the drinks went down smoothly. Porter wanted to check out the dance floor platforms. I didn't see anything wrong with going up the spiral staircase to see what was going on. Kaiden didn't seem to mind. Kaiden said he'd meet us up there and then left to go and refill our beverages. Porter and I loved being on the platform. We felt like V.I.P. We started dancing and enjoying letting loose.

Everything up until this point was going very well. It wasn't until I felt hands on my hips that all hell broke loose. What I thought were Kaiden's hands, were not. I had some man bumping and grinding on me. By the time I realized my mistake, it was too late to rectify the situation. Kaiden didn't like someone else's hands on me. He made that very well known. The guy was kicked out after Kaiden got a few punches in at his jaw. Bounce came to the rescue and led the guy to the door. I thought the night had been ruined. I turned my back once Bounce was on site. I wanted no part in watching. I stood at the railing and watched the people down below still partying and having a good time.

The music changed. The song was slower and very seductive. Kaiden's hands grabbed the railing on both sides of me. His arms caged me in. His body was close to mine. A hand dropped from the railing and came to my stomach. He pulled me closer to him. His body started moving to the beat and mine followed suit. Good this evening wasn't ruined after all. His free hand then came to my throat, he slid it up to my jaw. *"You are mine."* I titled my head and he kissed me. My god it was a kiss of ownership. I turned to face him when the kiss was broken. I put my arms around his neck. He put his hands on my ass. We slowly danced while making out. The song ended, but that didn't change the fact that he was groping my ass, his tongue was in my mouth or that my panties were getting wet. It was as if we were the only two in the place. The only thing that stopped us from getting in deeper was Bounce tapping on Kaiden's shoulder. He whispered something in his ear. Kaiden's demeanor changed instantly. He looked at me and told me he'd be right back. He told Bounce to stay with me and Porter until he got back. It annoyed me that he left his bouncer to babysit me. I watched Kaiden go down the spiral staircase and head toward the private door. I took off after him. I pushed and shoved my way through the crowd. I pulled that door open and it was dark. I ran down the dimmed red lit hallway. I reached Kaiden just as he was putting his palm to the keypad.

"I want to go with you."

"No, go back to Porter."

"I don't want to."

"I'm not asking, I'm telling you."

"What are you hiding from me?"

"Nothing. You saw what's behind door number two. Ciara, please just go back. I have to deal with a situation and then I want to get the hell out of here." I narrow my eyes at him. He cups my face and kisses me. *"Go and get Porter. I'll meet you at the front entrance."*

I really didn't want to walk away, but I did. I know there is more than what I saw going on on the other side of that locked door. Maybe not tonight, but I will get him to let me see.

CHAPTER NINE
KAIDEN

My blood was boiling when I saw that guy's hands on my girl. The way he was manhandling her pissed me off to no end. I could have seriously hurt that creep. If it weren't for Bounce, I would have done so. He should consider himself lucky I only got a few punches in on his face. I don't like men touching what isn't theirs to touch. I calmed down once I had Ciara back to myself. Having her warm, sexy body next to mine is a comfort I am not used to. Normally when I have a warm body in my arms, it's for sexual pleasure only. This feeling is new to me and I am liking it.

I was content slow dancing and kissing Ciara. Then when we got interrupted by Bounce, I wanted to scream, 'Christ, leave me the fuck alone. I am trying to build a relationship here.' I knew he had no choice once he told me what was going on. I had to take care of the problem. I've come to realize my clubs don't run smoothly without me here. I don't like that. I am really going to need to look at my employees. If by chance that I am the man for Ciara and we get married, I cannot be here all the time. I want to have a partner in life and maybe some kids in the future. I can retire whenever I want or sell. Until then, I need someone other than me to take some control for when I am not around.

I left Ciara up on the platform so that I could take care of the problem that arose. I was not happy she followed me. Ciara saw a glimpse into my other club, but there are things she did not see. If I allowed her to come with me, she would have seen what I am keeping from her. I can't let that ruin the wonderful evening we have been having. I know she didn't like it when I asked her to go and get Porter then wait for me by the door. I am sure she thinks I am an asshole, however, I did what is right for the both of us. I will make it up to her later.

When we got back to my house, Ciara went to her room and Porter went to the other spare bedroom. I came to my room, hoping that she would invite herself into my bed again tonight. I liked sharing my space with her. I didn't mind having a woman snuggle up next to me. I probably liked it too much.

As I unbutton my white dress shirt, all I can think about is wanting to unzip Ciara's dress for her. I want to watch her expression as it falls off her shoulders to the floor. The sound she makes when she gasps, I want to hear it fill the room. I let out a huff of air. I remove my shirt and drop it into the laundry bin. I leave my room and go to her door. It is open and she is laying on her bed still in her stunning dress, staring up at the ceiling. I walk in and crawl up unto the bed, covering her with my body. I take her hands and pin them to the mattress, then kiss her. God, she feels good underneath me.

"I want to devour your body," I whisper near her ear.

"I want to know what you are hiding from me behind door number two."

I got up to my knees, surprised she said that. She sits up and runs her fingers through my beard. *"You may look at me differently if you knew what goes on in Vibe's private club."*

"We can't build this relationship if you are hiding something from me." I get off the bed, facing away from her. I am battling what to do. Her hand touches

my bare back. *"Just tell me, Kaiden. Tell me what I don't know."*

I face her and take her hand in mine, bringing it up to my lips and kissing it. *"I'll show what you don't know."*

I hold her hand as we go to my bedroom where I get a key, then we go down the stairs, through the house, and out the back door. Ciara moves closer to me when we get outside. I lead her to a building on my property and unlock the door. I turn the lighting on that is automatically dimmed. I glance at her for her reaction when she comes inside. Her eyes are telling me that she didn't expect this. I hope I haven't scared her off. I wait for her to say something... anything. I watch her go further into my building. She wanders around looking and touching things that I am sure she's never used before. I want to run to her, pick her up and carry her out of here.

"What is this used for?"

"It's a spacer. It's to keep your legs spread."

Her eyes get big. *"Oh."* she puts it down. *"You are a dominant?"*

"Yes."

"Your club is like this?"

"Yes. I have members. My workers are not for sale."

"You want to use this stuff on me?"

"Yes, but only if you wanted me to."

"What if I don't like it?"

"Then we stop."

"What if we fall in love with each other and we see ourselves being together and I don't like it. Could you give this part of you up forever?"

"That is something I already thought about before placing my bid to date you. I wouldn't have gone through with this if I couldn't give this up."

"A zebra doesn't change its stripes."

"Good thing I'm not a zebra." She bites her lower lip. *"There is no difference if you think about it this way. You don't do the things I do. What if we do fall in love, could this be a part of your life if it meant being with me? One of us has to compromise if love wants to win."*

Ciara wanders around the room some more. She takes a whip off the wall. *"I'm not willing to have this used on me."*

"Then it would be gone."

She hangs it back on the wall. I watch her tread toward me. Her eyes stay fixed on mine. I wonder if she is going to bolt. She stands before me and inhales a deep breath. *"I am ready to see inside your world."*

"Are you sure?"

Her voice is soft when she says, *"Show me, Kaiden."*

I put a hand to her lower back and jolt her body to mine. *"When you didn't listen to me when I told you to stay with Porter. I wanted to punish you for following me and not listening."* I unzip her dress in the back, then I slide the straps down her arms. Her breasts are bare. Her nipples erect. I want to bite the pinkness. *"Are you ready to take your punishment?"*

"Yes."

I take her by the hand and she steps out of her dress that is now pooled around her feet. I bring her to the middle of the room. I lifted one of her arms at first then attached her wrist to a handcuff dangling from a chain attached to the ceiling. Then I repeat with her other wrist. Her hair sways across her back as she tilts her head back to see her confined wrists. I stagger over to the cabinets and turn some tempo music on low. I like hearing music that matches a woman's pulse. I go back to where I left Ciara. My palms are tingling as I see my beauty. My cock throbs with how sexy she is. I have to remember to control my excitement and go easy on her. This is her first time.

I stand behind Ciara. She peeks at me through her lashes over her shoulder. Her breath hitches when I grab her waist and bring her body to mine roughly. I place my hand to the front of her neck. I put my lips to her neck. They brush ever so lightly on her flesh as I talk.

"I was going to use my bare hand on your ass, but decided that you need a good lesson. You like to be rebellious and I can't have that." I bring the cat o' nine tails up to show her. I brush the ends over her breasts. She sucks in a breath. *"If at any time you need me to backoff tell me and I'll stop. Got it?"*

"Yes."

"Before we go any further, Ciara, do you trust me?" She nods her head. *"I need to hear you say it."*

"I trust you."

I step back from her and her body stiffens. I run the cat o' nine tails over her skin. She moans at the soft touch of the nine braided ropes. I swing my arm and it echoes as it smacks against her ass. She inhaled deeply. I do it again and again. I run my fingers over the pink lines. I check to make sure she's still with me. She hasn't told me to stop, but with fear, you sometimes forget you have a voice. I swung my arm again, the spanking was much harder. Her head falls back. Her lips part. Her eyes close. I keep going until her ass is bright pink. The marks visible. I drop the whip and I get to my knees. I kiss the marks I left. I then remove her thong. She presses her thighs together. I spank her ass with my hand, her legs spread back apart. I cup her pussy and run my finger along her lower lips. Her moan blends in with the music in the background. I stand and uncuff her wrists from above her head.

"How do you feel?"

"Was that it?"

"Not even close."

"Oh."

I swoop Ciara up in my arms and carry her over to the bed in the room. I place her on her back on the mattress. I undo my pants. My cock is fully engorged and free. Her lips part and her tongue darts out, licking her lips. I sit on the end of the bed. I reach out for her to take my hand. She yelps when I pull her body over my lap. I spank her ass and grab a handful.

"Do you know why I am spanking you, Ciara?"

"Because I didn't listen?"

"Wrong. It's because I didn't like that guy grinding on you. You are mine and only mine for as long as you are with me."

I spank her ass five more times. I feel her lower lips. I am satisfied they are wet. I spread her lips and entered her pussy with my fingers. I move my fingers inside her and spank her ass some more. Her hand fists the blanket. Her breathing becomes heavy.

The sounds coming from her mouth excites me more. My cock is throbbing. I wrap my arms around her waist and lift her from my lap. She watches me stroke my cock through lust filled eyes. I scoot to the head of the bed, putting my back to the headboard. She crawls to me, straddling my lap. I hold my shaft as she lowers herself onto my manhood. I groan as her pussy takes me. She rocks her hips and fuck she feels good. She holds onto the wooden headboard as I give her the control. Her pussy glides along my cock. Her moans are mixed with heavy breathing. I lean forward and kiss her neck. She throws her head back exposing more of her flesh to kiss, nibble and bite.

"Cum on my cock," I demand.

I grab her ass with both hands, moving her body faster. Her hands fall to my shoulders. Her grip gets tighter as she orgasms. I hold her back as I adjust our bodies and lay her to the mattress. I kiss her as I thrust back into her pussy. I fuck her deeply, wanting another orgasm from her before I give her mine.

"Fuck, Kaiden."

Her saying my name only makes me take her harder and faster. Her body stiffens before going limp. My cock is coated with her cum. I pull out and bring Ciara's mouth to my manhood. I groan while she sucks my cock until my orgasm releases in her mouth.

I fall to the mattress beside Ciara. She rolls over to her stomach and looks at me. Lust and desire are still prominent in her eyes. I reach over and tuck her hair behind her ear.

"Are you okay?"

"Mmmhmm." Her eyes blink shut.

I lean over and kiss her forehead. We are on the bed in the wrong direction, so I get up and get a blanket off the chair in the corner. I bring it to the bed and cover her before I get back on the bed. I watch her drift off to sleep. She is so incredibly beautiful.

CHAPTER TEN
CIARA

I woke about an hour ago and I slipped out of bed to use the bathroom. While I was in there, I checked out my ass. It doesn't look as bad as I thought it would. Only a few marks were left. I tiptoed around Kaiden's little building as he slept. I peeked into cabinets that I didn't look into last night. I saw some interesting things. I have to say, there are sex toys I have never used. Some of the things I had no clue what they are used for. I could guess, though. I have to admit, some of the things have me curious and a little excited. I wouldn't mind exploring Kaiden's lifestyle more. After last night, I now understand why he comes across as controlling. He is controlling. I just wonder why he has to be this way? What made him be a dominant man? Are people born this way or did something happen in their childhoods to make them be this way? I know I am not going to know unless he opens up to me.

I got back in bed with Kaiden. I watch him sleep as I lay here on my stomach. He seems so calm and at peace. I want to reach over and run my fingers through his well-kept hair that is a bit messy from sleep. I want him to wake so that I can learn more about this mysterious man. I have a feeling he hides a dark past that nobody knows about him. I don't think he allows anyone to get close enough to him to truly know who he is. I can see that with how cautious he is. It's almost as if he doesn't really trust anyone. If I am right, will he let me into all parts of his life? Will he trust me with his secrets?

"I can feel you staring at me."

I smile. *"I can't help it. You look so peaceful."*

He opens his eyes. *"You are a sight I could get used to seeing every morning."*

I cover my face with my hand. *"I look like hell."*

"No, sweetheart, you don't. You look as beautiful as ever."

I wrinkle up my nose. *"No need to be telling fibs."*

He lifts the blanket. I look. *"Does it look like I am fibbing?"* I hid my face in my arm that I'm laying on and giggled. Then I feel the blanket lift off my body.

His fingertips run over my ass. In a serious voice, he asks, *"Are you okay with last night?"*

I close my eyes. Kaiden's lips kiss the marks left behind. *"I am,"* I say as I inhale.

A moan escapes involuntarily. His fingers lightly brush the skin on the backs of my legs. My pussy tingles. I gasp when his fingers brush back up my inner thighs, all the way to my clit. I fist the blankets as he massages my sensitive nub. Good God his fingers are like magic. I yelp when I am suddenly flipped onto my back. I arch my back when he sucks my clit into his mouth. He enters his fingers inside of me as I grab a handful of his perfect, messy hair. I moan out his name as he plays with my pussy.

All too soon his fingers are gone, stopping an orgasm from coming. I let out a whimper. Kaiden flips me back over to my stomach. His body covers mine, pinning me to the mattress. He uses his knees to spread my legs apart. I gasped again when he thrust his hips and his engorged cock entered me. He slips a hand underneath me and finds my clit. Between his weight on me, his cock inside me, and his fingers playing with my clit, I can't breathe. I'm perfectly fine with it. I'm am so lost in the sex that I don't care.

"Fuck, you feel so good," he says, out of breath

himself. He jolts his manhood into me hard. I cum. He keeps thrusting through my orgasm. I moan when he groans, letting his own orgasm release. His head rests next to mine. *"I could do this all day."*

"Mmm, I'm not going to stop you."

Kaiden eventually rolls off of me. He catches his breath. *"I don't think Porter would appreciate us leaving him to fend for himself."* He smacks my ass before leaping from the bed. I watch him slip on his pants. Damn, I could stay here all day. He picks my dress up off the floor and brings it to me. I hope Porter doesn't see us come back to the house. He doesn't need to see me in last night's clothing with an orgasm glow on my face.

We drop Porter off at the airport. I am sad to see my friend go home and very sad to send Alaska with him. I know it's for the best. It's not easy to travel with a puppy. I know Porter will take good care of her for me. It does make me sad that I am going to miss her puppy days. Seven months is a long time to be away from her. I cross my fingers she doesn't forget who I am.

Kaiden had to stop by the club. He said he'd be

quick, so I stayed in the car. I wanted to take a few minutes to send a text to Warrick. Shay's birthday is tomorrow and I want to send her a gift. I had to make sure I sent it to the right place.

Kaiden gets back in the car. I can feel the anger seeping from his pores. I hear him say, what the fuck, under his breath as he looks at his phone in his hand.

"What's the matter?"

He looks out the windshield of the car. He ignores the question I ask him. He gets out of the car and I watch him jog to the news stand down the street. I squint my eyes hoping to see what he bought. He runs back to the car and gets back in. He hands me a tabloid and then pulls out into traffic. Horns honking behind us. I see the cover of the tabloid. My heart sinks and tears begin to fill my eyes. I stare at the picture. It's me and Kaiden dancing while making out. It's hot! That isn't why I have tears. I have tears because of the headline. 'Ciara Verbank moves on. Does Kaiden Marcellus know she's a slut?'

I watch out the passenger window as Kaiden speeds through Sin City. I try to stop crying but I can't. Someone is really trying to ruin me. I haven't helped the situation at all. I still haven't gotten ahold of Jacquelyn.

We pull into Kaiden's gated home. He parks out front instead of in his garage. *"I'll be right back."*

My tears dry up as I am getting angry. My phone chimes. I swipe the screen.

Hawk: I am going to sue that bitch. I am so sorry she is doing this to you.

Me: It's not your fault she is evil to the core.

My phone is going crazy!

Warrick: I'll be home tomorrow for her birthday.

Me: Okay!

Warrick: I saw the tabloid. Are you okay?

Me: I'm fine.

I lied. I am not fine.

Hawk: It is my fault, she worked for me.

Me: It's not like you have her stalking me.

Hawk: She'll be sorry she is doing this to you. I promise I'll take care of her.

I don't even know what to say to Hawk.

Hawk: I already have a plan to stop her.

Me: Don't do anything stupid, Hawk! You don't need trouble.

Hawk: Don't worry about me.

Warrick: I don't like what I read! I'll kick Kaiden's ass if he hurts you.

Now, I'm really mad!

Me: Why would you think Kaiden would hurt me?

Warrick: Read the article.

Kaiden gets back in the car. He sees my cell phone in my hand and takes it. I am shocked when he locks it in the glovebox. What the hell! Who does he think he is?

"Our day is not going to be disrupted by a fucking tabloid or by whomever you are texting with. I have something I want to show you."

I lean back in the seat. Juggling these men is exhausting. Then add this fucking psycho bitch and these tabloids to the mix, I want to block the world out. But, I am now curious about why Warrick is worried about me. What the hell was in that article I don't know about? I want to read it. I know Kaiden isn't going to allow that right now.

CHAPTER ELEVEN
KAIDEN

I have been driving so long that it is dark out. Ciara has fallen asleep. I park the car at the curb when we arrive at the destination. I reach into the backseat and get the tabloid. I turn on a light to read the shit someone printed. It isn't very long. I toss it to the backseat. I am glad whoever wrote this garbage believes they know me; not! There is no truth to anything they said about me. I am not going to pay any attention to what they think they know. I am strong enough of a man to ignore ignorance. Small minded people are annoying.

I run my knuckle down Ciara's cheek. She blinks her eyes and sits forward. *"Where are we?"*

"Come with me. I want to show you something."

I turn off the interior light and shut the engine off. I hear Ciara yawn. I get out and go to her side of the car, helping her out. I hold her hand as we approach the dark house. Ciara moves closer to me. Her free hand holds my arm. We step up onto the creaky front porch. The boards are old and weathered. I unlock the front door and step inside to turn a light on. The inside of the house is in much better condition than the outside.

"What is this place?

"This is where I grew up."

"Oh." I know this dump is nothing like the home I have now.

"My mother was a single mom. She worked hard to provide this place."

"What about your father?"

"Never knew him."

"Wow, I'm sorry."

"My mom always told me she wasn't sure who fathered me. She became ill with an autoimmune disease when I was nineteen. I was out of the house by then. I had moved to Sin City to be somebody. It's hard being someone of importance. I sold drugs to make a lot of money fast. I got busted so I stopped. I learned my lesson. By this time I was twenty-one, I had enough money to buy my club. I was on my way to come pick my mom up when I got a phone call from the neighbor. My mom passed away."

"Oh, Kaiden, I'm so sorry."

"I've been on my own ever since. Now, these past couple days, I have you. It's been rocky, but I love being with you. I don't know how I am going to say goodbye when the month ends."

"It won't be easy for you or me. We still have weeks to be together."

I bring her to me and kiss her. *"I look forward to every second."*

"Me too."

"Want to see my room?" I wink, being playful to change the mood.

"Absolutely!"

"I know it's not much to see. My mom didn't own this place. She rented. A few months after she passed, the house went into foreclosure. I bought it dirt cheap."

"It's not the price that matters, it's the memories."

"Yeah."

I take Ciara to my old bedroom. It's very small. Christ, my closet is bigger. I sit on the bed while she glances around. When I bought this place all of our stuff was still here. The owner didn't have the decency to let me in after her death, then he didn't even clean the place out. Asshole!

Ciara comes over to me and straddles my lap. Her fingers comb through my hair. She kisses me and damn this woman is getting to me. I don't want to let her go… ever!

She opens up to me about her mother and how Millie raised her. *"Your mom didn't have any more children?"*

"She did actually. I just never knew about it."

"What do you mean?"

"When I took possession of this house, I went looking through her stuff, looking for photos. I came across a photo album I'd never seen before. I saw pictures of a boy who looked just like me with a man I didn't know. I read the backs and their first names were on it. Tucked in the back was a Christmas card. I didn't know the family. I thought, hell, maybe I have an aunt or uncle I didn't know. I went to the address on the card. It wasn't an aunt or uncle. The kid that looked like me was my twin brother."

"Why would she say she didn't know who your father was?"

"The guy, my father, was shocked. He thought I was a con artist or something. He hired a private investigator to get answers. We learned my mother never told him she was pregnant with twins. He took my mother to court to get custody of my brother. He

won. So apparently, she gave him my brother and kept me a secret from him."

"Wow! That's crazy."

"Yeah, I guess having one baby was better than not having either one of us."

"Do you still talk to him?"

"No, I don't talk to my brother or my father. That's another story I don't want to get into right now."

I slide my hands up into her shirt when she presses her lips to mine. *"Hmm,"* she moans into my mouth.

"You make me want to do so many things to your body."

"You make me want you to do so many naughty things."

"Let's get out of here. I booked us a hotel room a few miles from here. We can get room service."

"Okay."

Ciara gets off my lap. She gets down to her knees between my legs. She looks up at me with her hands on the button of my jeans, asking for permission. I give her a nod. She undoes my jeans and I push them down to my thighs. She strokes my shaft before taking my cock in her mouth. She licks the head, the length and then wraps her lips around the girth, taking me to the base. I close my eyes, enjoying the pleasure she is giving me. I open my eyes, I grip her hair and buck my hips, taking control. I fuck her mouth until I cum. Before I can grab her and give her an orgasm, she gets to her feet and goes to the door. She giggles.

"Are you coming?"

I get up and do up my jeans then chase her out of my old room. I can be a patient man. It's her that will receive the rewards later for what she just did. I already planned on having sex with her all over the hotel room.

CHAPTER TWELVE
CIARA

Kaiden and I are at a very nice hotel in his hometown far from Vegas. My heart melted for him when he was telling me about his mother. I wanted to wrap my arms around him and hug him when he said he had a twin brother he never got to know. I felt very sad for him. I can see now why he is so cautious and protective. He is probably scared that the carpet will get swept out from under him. I feel there is much more to this man and I can't help but feel like I want to show this man love. He made me do a one-eighty. I didn't want to fall for him. I know that disliking him is no longer an option. I am slowly losing myself to him.

Kaiden ordered us some dinner. He asked me what I wanted and I told him to pick for me. He seemed to really like that. I'm sure I fed into his domineering ways. I am perfectly fine with that. A man should know what a woman likes, right? I know we don't know a lot about each other, yet, but it's a good way to learn. At least that is how I feel. The display of food he put out for breakfast, I am prepared to see half the menu brought up to our room.

"I have never been this far away from the club for this amount of time."

"Are you nervous something might happen while you are gone?"

"Kind of. I didn't even tell Jackie or Bounce that I wouldn't be in town. I guess this will be a good test for when I start taking time off."

"It's hard to stop doing what you love. I miss my shop and designing new clothes."

"Do you see yourself slowing down after all this?"

"I don't want to give it up if that is what you want to know. Going through this process, I see that I was missing out on some key factors in life. I was missing out on being in a happy, healthy relationship. What about you? Are you going to be able to slow down to be in a relationship?"

"If the relationship is with you, then yes. I might even consider selling. We live on separate sides of the

world. One of us would have to move if we are destined to be together."

"If you saw me before, why didn't you talk to me or ask me out? Why did you wait until my Grams did this?"

"Your beauty got my attention and I wanted to ask, but I wasn't in the right place to be asking you out on a date. If one date turned into more dates, I didn't have the time to dedicate myself to you or a relationship."

"But you do now?"

"I am all in, Ciara. I can see a future with you. It may be crazy to see that so soon into knowing each other. I feel we make a good match. I believe we would balance each other." He pauses. *"Complete each other."*

I smile. I don't know what else to say. A couple of days ago I wanted to not like him and now, I want to love him. Could we really be that couple that balance each other? Kaiden stands and bends to kiss my forehead before he goes to answer the door. My stomach grumbles. I am so hungry. Kaiden wheels in a cart full of food. See, I knew I was right and had nothing to worry about. I am not going to starve with him around. He sets out the food and I laugh when he raises his brow at the sound of my stomach growling.

"By the sounds of it, I have not done my job right today. I should have fed you sooner." He winks at me. I love it when he is relaxed and can crack a joke. *"I took the liberty of ordering you and me chicken parm with pasta on the side. One of my faves. Then for dessert, vanilla ice cream with strawberries and chocolate."*

"Sounds wonderful."

"Personally, I can't wait for the dessert."

Mmm, his devilish smile gets to me. I was just about to ask him if we could skip dinner, but he went and put the ice cream in the room's mini-refrigerator. I guess dinner first.

The dinner was absolutely delicious. I am too full and won't be eating dessert any time soon. Kaiden wheels the cart out to the hall just outside our door. I get up and walk over to the large floor to ceiling windows. I look out at the lights lighting the city we are in. It's beautiful to see. I close my eyes briefly when he comes up behind me and holds me in his embrace. I lean my weight against his strong frame. We just stand here together in silence. It's nice. Moments pass by but it feels like it's at a standstill. I could get used to being in his arms forever. The only thing is, I still need a better understanding of his lifestyle before I can be with him. I need to know if I can do the things he desires. If I cannot bend to be what he wants, can he change who he is to be with me. We are running out of time. A month really isn't that long if you think about it.

"If you wanted to dominate me right now, how would you do it considering we are away from your building?"

"There are ways without having a sex room."

"Is it only for when I do something you don't approve of?"

"Are you thinking about doing something I don't approve of?"

"Maybe."

"My lifestyle isn't always about lessons or punishment. It's also about sexual pleasure."

"So, I don't have to be bad to experience the things you want to do to me?"

One of Kaiden's hands slid up from my waist to my breast. His breath is hot on my neck. *"Do you want me to control your orgasm, Ciara?"*

"Yes," slips out of my mouth without a second thought of what that really means.

"I am going to strip you of your clothes."

I squeeze my thighs together. Just knowing his hands are going to be on my body is thrilling. When he lifted my shirt up, I didn't think he meant stripping me right here at the window. My pussy tingles with the thought of not knowing if anyone could see us. It's scary and exciting mixed together. My shirt falls to the floor, then my bra follows suit. I can hear my pulse beating in my ears as he removes my pants and undies. He lifts my hands and puts them to the glass above my head. I gasp as he puts his hand to my back and pushes my body to the cool window. My nipples are instantly erect and chills course through me. He then puts my forehead to the glass as well. Kaiden spreads my feet apart.

"Don't move."

I can tell he left me. The heat from him is gone. I wait for what is to come next. I want to close my legs as my pussy gets wet, wanting attention. I almost close them to give a reason for punishment. I fight to keep them spread apart as I want to experience this without defying him.

"Pick your head up." I do as I am told. He covers my eyes with cloth. A strap of some kind. *"I am getting undressed."* I bit my lip. *"My cock is so hard, Ciara."*

I wait for him to touch me… to fuck me… or do

whatever he wants to do with me. *"Oh, fuck, this feels good."* What is he doing? What feels good? *"I wish you could see me stroking myself while gazing at your sexy body."* He's getting himself off by looking at me? That's hot! But, so not fair. I want to rip this blindfolded off and watch him. A hand slips down the glass. *"Was that movement I saw, Ms. Verbank? Are you wanting to touch yourself?"*

"No, yes."

He puts my hand back where it was. *"Don't move it again."* He leans his forehead on my shoulder. He groans. This is driving me crazy. I want to touch him. I want his hands on me. I want his manhood inside of me right now. Goddamn it, I want his orgasm to be mine. I moan when his hand comes between my legs. *"Mmm, nice and wet for me."* I want more than ever to close my legs to keep his hand right there. His fingers enter me. *"Don't cum."* I don't know if I can stop that from happening. His fingers feel too good.

His breathing gets heavier. My body gets more tense. I am on the verge of an orgasm. I don't know if I can do as he told me. My hand slips again. I whimper when he removes his hand from my pussy. I hear him groan, then I feel his orgasm on my skin. The next thing I know he takes the blindfold off.

"Are you ready for dessert?" What!? Is he joking

right now? No way can he leave me in this state. That is not fair.

I push off the window. I am irritated. *"No!"*

"Are you sure? Because my mouth waters for it." I narrow my eyes at him. I don't move from my spot. I watch as he happily goes to get dessert from the freezer. He stares at me when he comes back and sits on the sofa. His voice is strict when he says, *"Ciara, come over here!"* I don't move from my spot. *"Now is not the time to be rebellious."*

I shrug a shoulder. He gets up and comes charging after me. I yelp when he picks me up and carries me to the sofa. He puts me on my ass then flips me over. His hand spanks my ass a few times. I moan. *"More."*

"You are testing my patience." He picks me up again and I land on my back. I try to get up but he stops me. *"You may not want dessert, but I do."*

Kaiden turns and picks up the vanilla ice cream. He gets a scoop and drops the spoonful on my nipple. I suck in a breath at the coldness. He gets the chocolate syrup and pours it over top. He then placed a strawberry on top. He watches my reaction. My chest is pumping hard. I keep my mouth shut. He picks the strawberry up with his teeth and brings it to my mouth. I bite it. He then begins to lick the ice cream off my nipple. Ugh, this man is seriously driving me crazy.

Kaiden kisses me and his fingers find my clit. I'm already a withering mess that I could cum at any second. Just when I could release, he stops. He brings me to a sitting position and spreads my legs to be in between them. He grins when he gets more ice cream from the bowl, making himself a sundae on my other breast. When he licks that one clean off, he kisses me again. I moan into his mouth as his cock penetrates me. Kaiden takes his sweet time fucking me. His cock fills me only to take it away. I get irritated more. I sit up and grab his face.

"Stop fucking with me and make me cum."

He pulls my lower body practically off the sofa. He slams his manhood inside me. I grab the edge, brace myself for more. I want more. He holds my hips and thrusts harder into me. I take what he's doing to my body. I welcome his assault. I love it, really.

I orgasm saying his name. He slams his cock into me as far as he can go and he groans as he orgasms, too.

When the orgasm subsides, he removes himself from inside me. *"Best fucking dessert I have ever had."*

CHAPTER THIRTEEN
CIARA

I woke up this morning knowing this is the day I have to leave Kaiden. I don't like it. Kaiden and I had a bit of a rocky start, but once we got over the hump, we really got along very well. I didn't end up hating him like I wanted. Nope, I fell for the guy - hard! It is breaking me inside that I have to break up with him. I honestly do not want to leave him. How in the hell did this happen? How did I fall for that guy that is so very much different than I? I don't even care how it happened, honestly. I just want to stay with him.

When he opened his past to me that is when it really began. He hasn't stopped sharing with me ever since. The only thing he didn't talk about was the father and brother he doesn't know. I wanted to share, but that is the one thing he kept to himself. My heart breaks for him and I wish he would have opened that part of him.

After we came back from his hometown, we spent a few days at his home. We didn't go anywhere. I have to admit, we had a lot of sex. It wasn't always in his building. He does have a tender loving affectionate side. We made love multiple times. I'm not going to hide the truth we spent many nights out in his building.

We did go to Vibe quite a few nights. Kaiden really likes to show me off and makes sure that everyone knows I am off limits. I was his and that's all there was to it. One night while we were there, he did take me further behind door number two. I saw some of the rooms. I saw the list of members. Now that I have seen into his world, it didn't bother me what the "real" Vibe is. I was super excited when we actually used one of the rooms. Sex with Kaiden is different than what I have had with the other guys and definitely different than past boyfriends. I enjoyed every second of it. I am not sure how I can go back to how I did things before. But, I guess I may not have a choice. Just as I don't have the choice of staying with Kaiden. Well I have a choice, but that is six more months from now.

I am packing my suitcase when Kaiden comes

into his bedroom. I look him in the eyes. I see the same pain as I saw when he was telling me about his mother. I hate that I'm the reason it's there. I want to run into his arms and tell him to not let go of me. I want him to demand that I stay. I don't run into his arms, though. I finish packing my clothes. I watch him out of the corner of my eye when he goes to the closet.

"You forgot this." It's the dress he bought me. The one that I actually made.

"I'm leaving that here."

"Why? You don't want it?"

"I want you to keep it. Maybe when you see it, you'll think about me."

"Ciara, look at me." I do. *"I'll be thinking about you until you come back to me."*

"I wish you would have asked me out when you first saw me, then we wouldn't be going through this stupid breakup."

"Don't think of it as a breakup, think of it as putting us on pause."

I turn away from him. *"Please, keep the dress for me."*

"Are you all set to go?"

"I guess so."

"Your car is waiting."

Tears fill my eyes. Here I go, crying like I always do. Goddamn it, this pisses me off. Kaiden puts an arm around my waist and spins me to face him. *"Kaiden."* I say as I fall into his warm embrace.

"Just come back to me. I want to be with you. I am head over heels crazy for you."

He kisses the top of my head. I lift my head and put my arms around his neck. *"I can't do this. I cannot leave with you watching me."*

"Then I will go."

I kiss him with all the emotions inside of me. I reluctantly step away from him. He gets my suitcase and starts walking toward the door. I follow him out of his bedroom after I take one more glance around his space. We get to the front door. He sets my luggage down.

"This isn't goodbye, so I'm not going to say it. See you in six months."

I cry when he walks out his front door. I start to chase after him. I stop myself. I see him get in his car and zoom off. I close my eyes wishing he'd come back. I wait to hear the car's engine, but it doesn't come. The only sound is a man's voice asking if I am ready. Fuck no I'm not ready, the voice inside my head screams. I manage to nod my head. He takes my luggage to the car.

The reality sets in that May is only a day away. A new man is going to enter my life. I am not going to pretend that I'm happy about it. Hell, I'm not even going to pretend that I won't like the next guy. We see how well that worked out for me.

Where the hell has Grams been hiding these guys. Why didn't she introduce me to one or two of them before now? Why the hell is she doing this to me all at once?

The driver stops on the strip and tells me we are here. What does he mean we are here? I'm not leaving Vegas? I open my carrier bag and take out the three-ring binder. Sure enough, I'm not leaving Vegas. Tomorrow I am supposed to meet Gaetano Stagnitto. I look at the hotel before me, Seven Jewels. I exhale a deep breath. I let out a laugh before bursting into tears.

"Take me back to Kaiden's," I yell at the driver.

"No can do, ma'am, I have orders to make sure you check-in at this hotel."

"Fuck you." I get out and go to the back of the car to wait for my belongings. When the driver sets it down, I wheel it into the hotel. I'm going to my room and I'm not leaving.

ABOUT THE AUTHOR

Thank you so much for taking the time to read Grandma's Silent Auction April. Word-of-mouth is crucial for any author to succeed. If you enjoyed the book, please leave a review on Amazon. Even if it's just a sentence or two. It would make all the difference and would be very much appreciated. – OXOX Michael James

Website: http://michaeljames-author332.bravesites.com/

ALSO BY MICHAEL JAMES

If you enjoyed Grandma's Silent Auction April, you may also like my other books:

The Way We Love series:

Pink Skies At Night

Shadows At Night

Nights Are Unlimited

Concealed By The Night

Shattered At Night

Freed At Night

Winning A Cowgirl's Heart - Trilogy:

The Rodeo King

The Best Friend

The Fate Of My Heart

Winning a Cowgirl's Heart -Complete Box Set

Construction Vs. Corporate- Trilogy:

Unbalanced

Balancing

Balanced

Secrets Within a Club

Club Comrade

Revenge

Saving Club Conrad

Masquerade Saga

His Pearls

His Secrets

His Prison

His Games

His Moves

All His

Crime in Landkaster series

The Mirror

Times Like These

Lonely Road of Faith

Grandma's Silent Auction series

January

February

March

Standalone:

Toying With October

Pieces Of Me

A Christmas For Eve

Dom Diaries: Tangled Up In You

Christmas Scavenger Hunt

Blue Christmas

Stealing the Christmas Spotlight

Co-written with Jodi Fahey

Last Sheet

Book 2

Book 3

Manufactured by Amazon.ca
Bolton, ON

44035022R00061